I0782193

Turbulent Justice

BY

Eidahs

COVER & EDITING BY

BINKY INK

BINKY INK

THE LITERARY ARM OF BINKY PRODUCTIONS

WWW.BINKYPRODUCTIONS.COM/SHORTSTORIES

Turbulent Justice Copyright © Binky Ink 2025

All rights reserved. No part of this book may be reproduced in any form or by any electronic or mechanical means, including information storage and retrieval systems, without written permission from the author, except in the case of the reviewer, who may quote brief passages embodied in critical articles or in a review.

This is a work of fiction. Names, characters, places, and incidents either are the product of the author's imagination or are used fictitiously, and any resemblance to actual persons, living or dead, events, or locales is entirely coincidental.

Published in 2025 by Binky Ink
Cover and Editing by Binky Ink

ISBN: 978-1-998701-00-1

<u>WARNINGS:</u>

Violence, Blood, Vomiting.

Table of Contents

Luke and Zach stepped up to the coffee shop door, and as per, tried to enter the narrow doorway at the same time.

'You got us stuck again,' Zach complained, his bushy eyebrows furrowing in annoyance as a lock of his black hair made its way down to his eyes.

'Na-ah!'

Luke recalled that last time *maybe* it was him, but it wasn't him this time. He was preparing his elaborate defence when Zach reached over to pick at Luke's face.

'You have a fleck of something.'

Luke squirmed his face away, chuckling. Luke's tan-beige skin meant fluffs always stuck out, unlike with Zach's much paler complexion. His eyes were so vivid in comparison to Luke's brown eyes, Luke could get lost just staring into them.

Square jaw set as Zach focused on Luke, Luke couldn't help but feel even more affection for him.

'This your way of making up for coming home so late?'

Zach's bright blue eyes widened before he averted his gaze. 'I was following a lead.'

'I hope you clocked in overtime,' said Luke.

'It was . . . a dead end.' Zach's eyes grew distant, the look he got when he was reliving something in his mind. Then he smiled at Luke, and warmth bloomed in Luke's stomach. Zach's next words reverberated in his throat with that hoarse conviction that made him so sexy. 'I would do anything for you, you know that?'

'Zach,' Luke said softly, his heart swelling. 'Where is this coming from?'

Their anniversary wasn't for months yet. While things were comfortable after all their time together, that comfort never detracted from the intensity of what Luke felt for Zach. Luke never took Zach for granted. As such, every day was like an anniversary to him, and their actual anniversaries felt just as special as those spontaneous moments Luke so cherished. It was a feeling he never thought he'd experience again, not after losing Harry.

The barista walked over to them, glancing at the badges clipped onto their belts. 'Morning Detectives.' She met their gazes. 'You're blocking my entrance.'

Zach rolled his eyes and Luke sighed. Squeezing through, they both entered the coffee shop proper. Luke swiped a lock of his brown hair out of his face, suppressing a laugh.

'Will your order be to go?' the barista asked. The detectives confirmed and made their orders. 'The way you partners act, one would think you were either brothers or married.'

They both froze, staring wide-eyed at each other. Luke couldn't stop the grin that spread across his face. Zach blushed and averted his gaze.

'Oh, I'm sorry. You just act like you're more than investigative partners, I just assumed.'

It was Zach who confirmed. 'We are both. Partners in all things in life.' He smiled cheekily at Luke. 'You were at the firm when I started there.'

'Of course I was there before, I'm a whole decade older than you. I was made your partner so I could train you. We make too good a team . . . everywhere.' Luke thought of their morning – of the ferocious passion Zach had exuded the minute he'd entered the bedroom – and felt his face warm.

'Married, eh,' Zach repeated wistfully. He bit his lip nervously.

'I mean, I'm not opposed to it.' Luke grimaced – that had sounded terrible. 'I mean, it's just . . . Harry . . .'

Luke had lost his husband and never thought he'd love like that again. Luke was mad about Zach, every day he felt the flutters of their love. And Luke didn't care that Zach was ten years his junior. Luke was forty-three now, though, and while he was committed to Zach, getting married now . . . There were so many suppressed fears Luke had never openly addressed.

Zach took Luke's hands in his. 'I get it, you're a widower.' Zach's gaze dropped to his feet.

'You know what that kind of loss feels like,' Luke said gently. Zach too had lost the man he loved.

Zach nodded. 'Do you remember what I told you when I started working with you?' Zach asked suddenly, his voice filled once more with conviction.

'You said you were going to bring justice to the world because it had failed the man you loved. And I said I was still pursuing it because a mistake I made led my husband to be murdered.'

'We promised we would see it through together,' said Zach. 'It was a vow. That's why—'

Both their phones began blaring. Glancing at both their screens, Luke knew Zach had received the same message. *Murder vic found.* The address of the crime scene followed.

Luke and Zach took their coffees and left quickly in their vehicle. As Luke turned onto the freeway, he glanced at Zach.

'We got interrupted. You were about to add something.'

Zach smiled mildly. 'It's fine. Let's see this justice done together first.'

Luke reached over to squeeze Zach's thigh. 'When I say I'm not opposed, I mean to say that I just need to process emotions because I'm a widower. I *do* want a long future with you, Zach. Heck, we've been together nearly a decade – of course, I want our relationship to last. Every day with you feels like a miracle because . . . Every time we get a new case, every time we might be risking our lives, it's as though not being married will protect me from the hurt because . . .'

Luke kept his focus on the freeway traffic, his heart racing from admitting all these conflicting emotions. Zach waited for Luke to continue.

'I am . . . scared,' Luke finally expressed. 'Scared to lose you too.'

It was Zach's turn to reach over and squeeze Luke's thigh. He spoke softly. 'I have that fear too. Which is why I understand.'

The two remained silent until they arrived at the crime scene. Luke took hold of Zach by the arm to stop him before they entered.

'I do want to.' Luke confirmed.

Hope and sadness warred on Zach's face. 'Tell me that again if you still want to tomorrow.'

Luke breathed out a small laugh. 'A good twenty-four hours after the topic came up? You using my own wisdom on me now? Fine, we can reassess when—'

'When we've solved this case.' Zach marched into the house. Luke followed.

The scene was simple, clean. The victim, a man in his thirties, had a stab wound to the neck, located in the right spot to guarantee almost instant death. Preliminary reports from the forensics team claimed there was no evidence left behind by the murderer, except for a calling card on which was written *3 of 4*. Beside it was a note, a cryptic message with jumbled letters one had to decipher –a computer at the office would decipher it within seconds.

Swallowing the uncomfortable lump in his throat that seeing a dead body always garnered, Luke looked up from the note and at Zach. His partner's eyes were scrunched with chagrin, staring away from the victim.

Luke took his hand. 'Hey, it's okay. You . . . you used to always get like this at crime scenes, but it stopped after a while. Is . . . there something about this scene that brings back those dark memories for you?'

'The stab wound.' A tear ran down Zach's face. Luke instinctively wiped it away with his thumb, his heart wrenching for Zach. 'That is where Kieth—' Zach put a hand to his mouth. 'When he killed himself.'

Luke had his arms around Zach in an instant, stroking the back of his neck and whispering words of understanding in soothing tones. When he pulled away, Zach had fire in his eyes.

'We have to see this through to the end together, Luke.'

'And we will. Now,' Luke pointed at the calling card. 'Three out of four. We're a bit out of order here. We need to find one, two, and four. If this is the third of four murders, I am guessing our killer got all four already. And that this was premeditated.'

Zach tilted his head towards the note. 'That might give us a clue.'

'Let's bring it down to the station to decipher. I am not spending brainpower I need to find a murderer on a riddle like this.'

Zach chuckled mildly. 'Bet you once deciphered, it *is* a riddle.' He was diffusing, Luke knew, but it got him chuckling all the same.

Luke clicked his tongue and hissed, but smiled when he saw Zach give him a wan smile.

They proceeded to examine the murder scene. Their forensic pathologist collected the body to bring it in ahead of the detectives, and now Luke and Zach were on their way to headquarters.

They were nearly there when their boss, Melinda Grayson, called in. Luke put her on the car's speakers. 'Did a background check on our vic.'

Luke scowled. 'And?'

'Our murderer is cleaning the streets, it appears,' said Melinda. 'This guy, the vic, has been to prison on multiple charges and is a known sex offender. Oh, and we found a tattoo we think is significant.'

'Significant how?' asked Luke

'I . . . well . . . you see . . .' It wasn't like Melinda to stumble on her words, and it made Luke's heart palpitate.

'Send over an image of the tattoo,' Luke told her.

'I really think you should wait to see it when you arrive here at H.Q.'

'Why?' demanded Luke. 'What's going on, Melinda?'

'That's Chief Investigator Grayson, and—'

'The image, now!' Luke knew there was more to it and he wanted to find out now.

Zach's hand found his on the steering wheel. 'Slow down.'

Luke realised he was way past the speed limit. He slowed the car as the image of the tattoo came in. Then slammed on the brakes abruptly, his chest tight, feeling unable to breathe anymore.

<u>PART 2</u>

Within seconds, Zach was rubbing Luke's back and guiding his breathing. Luke was trembling from head to toe.

He looked back at the image of the tattoo on the screen and his vision blurred. He got out of the car, slamming the door shut, and leaned against it for support, bringing his hand to his eyes as tears poured down his face.

Zach joined him, wrapping his arms around him.

'This can't be happening.' Luke heaved. 'This is all bringing it back.'

'It's okay. I'm here.'

Luke heaved again. 'That tattoo, the human skull with the antlers with a reversed pentagram below it . . . that was . . .' Luke scrunched his face in fury. 'That symbol was left behind at the crime scene when Harry was murdered.'

'Then one of the murderers has been found,' Zach soothed. His voice took an edge, 'And eliminated.'

Luke pulled away. 'You don't understand, Zach. Those people who killed him, it was always evident it was a group of four, they made that clear, and they always left behind that symbol painted in their victims' blood.'

'Then it makes sense they would have it tattooed on themselves,' stated Zach.

'The first time they killed, we thought we'd found their leader – *I* thought I'd found their leader. In the end, we convicted the wrong man.'

Zach swallowed, his jaw tight as he nodded.

Luke furrowed his brows. 'They killed again.' The memory hit Luke in the gut. 'Their third victim was Harry.'

'I know.' Standing in a wider stance, it felt like Zach's entire body was wrapped around Luke. Luke was broader than Zach, but the lean man always knew how to envelop Luke into his embrace. Zach ran circles with his thumbs over Luke's face – it was comforting.

'Despite leaving their own messages at the scenes, the killers never left any evidence behind and we never found them.' Luke pondered. 'It has to be a coincidence.'

'Does it? The calling card said *3 of 4*. I have to wager a guess someone has found the murderers who killed your husband.'

'How could someone have found them when *I* could not?' Luke pleaded. 'I searched for years! If *I* couldn't find them, how could someone else?'

'Maybe they got lucky,' Zach offered.

Luke met his partner's gaze, the tenderness in them making him nearly forget the hurt that had just re-surfaced from the grief of his loss. He pressed a hard kiss to Zach's lips, which was reciprocated with fervour.

Luke whispered a soft 'Thank you' when he pulled away.

Luke took a beat to recompose himself. 'Okay, I'm good.' Zach nodded and both got back into the car.

Once at H.Q., Melinda was apologetic but speaking in her usual matter-of-fact tones, updating Luke and Zach on her analyses.

'Well, we still need to decipher that message left behind by the murderer,' concluded Luke. He stopped, turning to face Melinda. '*Could* this be linked to those murders thirteen years ago?'

Melinda shrugged. 'The vic *could* be one of those murderers.'

Luke shook his head. 'I failed to find them. I had the wrong guy. Because of that mistake, it got Harry killed.'

Zach had his hands on Luke's shoulders and was staring deep into his eyes before Luke took his next breath.

'Harry's death is not your fault. The evidence led you to the wrong guy because those murderers were that good at what they did. None of what happened back then is your fault, *none of it.*'

There was something in the way Zach spoke. Luke furrowed his brows. Then it hit him like a slab of concrete as realisation surfaced.

'The guy I convicted, his name was *Kieth* Stewart. He killed himself in prison.'

Zach's eyes sparkled with fresh tears.

Luke gasped. 'Zach, why did you never tell me?!' Luke was wracked with guilt. 'I got him killed too.

Because of me, the man you loved died.' He felt like an idiot for missing the obvious. 'I . . . never connected the dots before.'

'Because I didn't *want* you to connect those dots – I wasn't ready. Because . . .' Zach took a steadying breath. When he spoke, again his voice was soft and soothing.

'Listen, I hadn't realised you'd been the one to investigate the murder until way into our first year together.' Zach cupped Luke's face with both hands. 'I don't blame you for Kieth's death and never have. You are not responsible for either of their deaths.' Zach pointed behind him, raising his voice. 'Those *maniacs* are. You got that? *You* are *not* at fault and *I don't blame you.*'

Luke couldn't meet Zach's gaze.

Luke had followed the evidence. Weapons with the accused's fingerprints had been found at the scene of the crime, weapons the accused claimed had been stolen. A lie detector test showed Kieth had been lying about something, or at least that's what they had all believed at the firm because they wanted to believe the atrocity and gruesomeness of the gang murder would be brought to justice.

When Luke realised his mistake, when a second crime scene with the same emblem came to light, it was already too late, Kieth Stewart had been convicted for life and had killed himself in prison. Luke had been blaming himself for that man's death and for Harry's death all these years.

The murderers, whom the firm had dubbed the Skull-Star murderers, had continued for several years, all grotesquely painting their victim's walls in their blood with their symbol, later on revealing they were four forming a ritualistic circle.

These gang murders had stopped after a time. Useless clues left behind by the perpetrators indicated a pact between them, thus if the crimes had stopped, Luke had surmised it was because one or more of the murderers was indisposed to conduct their atrocities.

The Skull-Star murderers had killed over a dozen people in this way, somehow never leaving any trace of D.N.A. or fingerprints at the crime scenes.

Harry had put up more of a fight than some, being a private investigator and crime detective, but in the end, the four killers had gotten him too. Luke was the one who found him. Harry had been preparing their anniversary dinner. His death was on their wedding anniversary. It would forever haunt Luke.

'Are you with me, Luke? Stop swimming in the past. At least, stop thinking you are at fault.'

Luke was brought back by Zach's soft-spoken words. All he could do was stare into the other man's vivid eyes. Zach whispered. 'I love you.'

Luke blinked a few times, regaining his composure. He realised Melinda was looking on and a touch of embarrassment came over him.

'Listen, if this case is too much for either of you, given the circumstances . . .' She trailed off. She had never chided Luke and Zach for their relationship, but had always warned them to take a step back from a case if it got too heavy for either of them or caused strain between them.

'No. I want to see this through, see if the four victims are our Skull-Star murderers.'

'I am committed to this all the way through,' Zach confirmed.

Melinda nodded, and the three of them proceeded to run the coded message through the system.

It read: *All four have been found and confirmed.*

'That answers *that* question,' said Zach. And Luke knew it to be true – this victim was one of the four murderers to have killed Harry and gotten Kieth falsely accused.

Luke met Zach's fiery gaze. 'We need to find the other three.'

<u>Part 3</u>

The call was put out to be on alert for anyone found dead with a stab wound to the neck. As previously speculated, it was likely all four were already dead.

It didn't take long before another body matching their criteria was found and reported to the firm.

Luke and Zach arrived at the scene which was in full swing. Forensics was processing the scene while the pathologist was doing preliminary examinations of the body.

As cameras flashed in the dim room to capture the angles of the victim's neck wound, Luke flashbacked to when he found Harry. The team had processed him while Luke had stood in shock for an hour before collapsing to his knees in sobs.

A loud swallowing sound brought Luke's attention to Zach, whose lips were pressed together in a straight line. He was staring at the stab wound in the victim's body. Luke realised Zach was trembling.

Forgetting his own turmoil, Luke took one large stride to Zach and placed a hand on his arm. 'Zach, you with me? You okay?'

Zach merely nodded. It wasn't like him to fall so silent like this. Luke was worried about his partner.

'You'd tell me if there was more?' Luke asked.

Zach snapped his gaze abruptly to Luke, his eyes filled with pleading and glistening with tears. His jaw was set tight.

Luke furrowed his brows. 'Zach, talk to me. What's . . .' He placed a hand on Zach's chest. His partner's heart was beating faster and harder than his.

'Let's just find the other bodies.'

'Okay.' Luke bent down to peer at the calling card. 'Two on four. They've got that right.' He studied the second note. He checked on his phone for the result of the deciphered first note, the one that was the third in the series of notes.

Luke took the few needed minutes to decipher this second note himself. It read: *Looking deeper into it led to the truth.*

'Well, that's what we're doing.' He offered Zach a wan smile, but the other man remained fixed on the victim's neck.

Luke walked over to their pathologist to ask the question he knew Zach was as eager to learn the answer to as *he* was. Indeed, the victim had the same tattoo as the other guy, the symbol that had given these criminals their name at the firm: Skull-Star.

Before Luke could decide or ask anything else, Zach was already marching out of the place and back to their car. Luke called after him to no avail.

Luke hurried out of the house to find Zach sitting in the passenger seat, hand on his mouth, his eyes distant.

With a pang, Luke got in the car and drove to the next crime scene, which had been reported in by Melinda during their examinations of the second victim. In fact, two such scenes had been reported in.

'We have two options,' said Luke. 'One north of downtown and the other south-east.'

'Let's go south-east first.' Zach answered quickly and without moving from his outward stare.

Luke offered Zach a smile, heartened that his partner had spoken, but Zach remained impassive, looking out the window.

Luke called in the scene they were going to next so the team would join them there once done at the other location. The fourth scene had been taped off by the cops who stood outside the building, but the crime scene itself would remain untouched until the detectives on the case – Luke and Zach – arrived.

When they reached the south-east location, it had already been confirmed that the victim, another male perpetrator with a history of violence, had a tattoo of the same kind – human skull with antlers, an upside-down pentagram beneath it.

Zach stepped out of the car first, making for the apartment building. Luke ran ahead and blocked his path.

'Okay, Zach, what's going on? Talk to me.' Luke was genuinely worried. With every scene they visited, Zach became increasingly distraught.

The sunset behind Zach created an orange back-drop, and Luke realised they'd been at it with this case all day. The hues on the horizon made Zach's eyes seem all the more bright, and all the more blue.

Zach, still looking like he was pleading, stared past Luke until he focused on his gaze.

Zach grabbed Luke's face, pressing him against the brick wall, and kissed him so fiercely, Luke forgot where they were or what they were doing. His legs were weak and he felt the flutters in his stomach as his lover kissed him with desperation, moans escaping the younger man's lips.

The moment's ferocity matched that of this morning's. Luke could only deepen the kiss, wanting more as both men glided their hands up and down their bodies, squeezing. Zach continued with abandon.

Luke tasted the saltiness of Zach's tears as he sobbed into Luke's mouth.

When Zach pulled away, Luke was breathless. Zach leaned his forehead on Luke's, weeping. 'I don't ever want to lose you, Luke. I need you. I love you.'

'Zach.' Luke tried to sound soothing. He wanted to ask what more this was about, but the day had been long and full of so many emotions for both of them, especially considering the circumstances.

Another choked sob escaped Zach.

'I love you, Zach.' Luke asserted. As Zach had done for him, Luke gently brushed the tears away with his fingers. Zach kept his trembling hands pressed against Luke's chest. Luke repeated in a whisper. 'I love you.'

Zach lunged for Luke's mouth again, eliciting a moan from the older man. The kiss screamed something was wrong, and Luke was helpless to do anything for the man he loved, so long as Zach didn't tell him what was going on in his mind.

Zach broke away and entered the building so abruptly, it left Luke feeling flustered, and a pang hit him.

Luke followed Zach up the stairs to the apartment where the team had begun processing the crime scene.

This time, instead of remaining tight-lipped, as soon as Zach saw the body, he bolted to the bathroom.

'Zach!' Luke hurried after him.

Zach slammed the door shut on Luke. Luke heard him sobbing heavily. He tentatively pushed the door open. Zach was leaning on the sink, hands gripping it tightly, heaving. Zach's tears weren't the only thing dripping from his face.

'Zach, you're sweating.'

Luke instinctively put a hand to Zach's forehead, checking for a fever. That's when Zach turned to the toilet and vomited. Wincing internally, Luke turned away.

Finally, after retching a few times more, Zach rinsed his mouth and face and stepped out of the bathroom with Luke. The older detective wanted to ask if this was too much, but he knew his partner would be stubborn. As it was, Zach answered before Luke had voiced anything.

'Just one more.' Zach repeated more softly, 'Just one more.'

Zach walked to the mantle where the calling card and note were placed. *One on four.* Zach's the one who deciphered the note. *A drunken night led to boasting of hidden tattoos.*

Luke put the message together in his mind before voicing it out loud.

A drunken night led to boasting of hidden tattoos.

Looking deeper into it led to the truth.

All four have been found and confirmed.

'Our killer's giving us their story,' Luke deduced.

'Just one more.' Zach looked up at Luke. 'Please.' It came out like a beg.

Zach took Luke's hand, interlacing their fingers, and led him out of the apartment and to the car. It was Luke's turn to remain quiet. Hands trembling, Zach got into the car.

Luke drove to the final location, ever worried for Zach and whatever was going through his mind or what he was feeling.

Luke himself was still reeling from Harry's death, the flashback so raw, but his love for Zach kept him going, kept him focused, with Zach's repeated words from this morning offering comfort. *Let's see this justice done together.*

While they were finding Harry's killers, their bodies were not as Harry had been found, but how Kieth had died. Luke knew this would be disconcerting to Zach – now that he'd put two and two together – but he hadn't realised just how much.

They arrived at the final location and stepped into an empty loft apartment. The scene had not yet been processed, as the team was still finishing up at the previous location. Melinda had cautioned them to leave things untouched until the team arrived if they got there beforehand.

Zach took a slow, deep breath and seemed calmer now. Still nervous, but that desperation had been replaced by something more akin to relief. And something else, something inscrutable.

Luke studied the note. The calling card stated *Four of four.*

Luke stared down at the note, deciphering it in his mind. Something about it made his heart race in trepidation. *Now justice has been made for the men they took from us.*

It made no sense, some of this foursome's victims had been women. The phrasing, Luke realised, was reminiscent of something Zach had told him ten years ago.

Behind him, Zach swallowed loudly and let out a shaking breath.

The gears started turning in Luke's mind.

I'm going to bring justice to the world because it failed the man I loved.

You are not responsible for either of their deaths. Those maniacs are.

The stab wound in the neck, that was how Kieth had killed himself. And all these murderers, now victims of murder themselves, had a knife jabbed into their necks.

Now justice has been made for the men they took from us.

That's when Luke realised who had murdered these murderers.

A pang hit Luke in the gut. His grip on the note faltered and it fell to the floor. He slowly turned to Zach, whose eyes were sparkling.

'You said we'd see this through together,' Luke said carefully. 'This is what you meant?' His voice cracked.

'I'm sorry,' Zach whispered.

Instinctively Luke reached for his gun, but Zach was faster and he kicked the gun out of his hand. It went skittering across the floor.

Heart pounding, Luke stared at the man he loved.

Zach pressed his lips together as his tears fell. 'It's over, Luke.'

<u>PART 4</u>

'It's over, Luke. They're dead. Justice for Kieth and Harry is made.'

Luke took a staggering step back, nearly tripping on himself. 'Are you going to kill me now?' The question came out before he could stop himself. He assumed the answer but he needed to hear the confirmation from Zach.

Zach looked confused. 'No. I can't lose you, Luke. I told you, I don't blame you for Kieth's death. I blame *them.*'

'You . . . You became a detective because of what happened to Kieth.' Cold gripped in Luke's stomach. 'You knew I was the one to convict him.'

Zach shook his head. 'Not when I joined the agency. We were partners first. I only learnt after a year of working together.'

'When? You've known for a decade and you never told me?!' Even as Luke shouted, he knew the truth. 'No,' he said more calmly, 'you might have omitted details, but you never lied about your intentions, your motives.'

He remembered one night in particular, the night of their first kiss.

* * *

Luke found Zach sitting on a park bench. 'There you are! You left rather quickly. What's going on, Zach? Talk to me.' Luke sat down beside him. 'Is this to do with the vic earlier today?'

Zach shook his head. 'It's still hard to witness a dead person, but I am . . . acclimatising to it.'

'It's okay to be sensitive about this. I always feel a lump in my throat when I see a body.' Luke hesitated. He asked gently, 'So what's upset you?'

'I learnt something today. It . . . was unexpected, and causes me turmoil. But at the same time, I am even more committed to bringing justice because of . . . for the men we lost.' Zach met Luke's gaze, fire in his eyes. 'I won't stop until it's done.'

'Just be sure to stay alive through it all,' said Luke. 'I've grown quite fond of you.' He felt his cheeks flush hot and quickly glanced away.

Zach smiled. 'We're going to see this through together. And . . . I've grown quite fond of you too.' He hesitated, biting his lower lip nervously. 'So how fond are we talking about exactly?' His eyes reflected hope and it fluttered Luke's stomach.

'Care for me to demonstrate?' Luke leaned in tentatively.

Zach's gaze turned fiery again. He leaned in fast to meet Luke, where they both hesitated. Luke closed the distance, and Zach deepened the kiss. Their kiss turned fierce, igniting a fire that to this day remained ablaze.

* * *

'You revealed the truth by hiding some of it,' Luke muttered. 'Why didn't you call it in when you found them? Before all this . . .' Luke gestured to the dead body.

'I followed them for months to be certain, bribed them and paid them to show me their tattoos. I searched for evidence, and found it, but it wouldn't have been enough for the courts. Not without a confession.'

'You still could have called it in.'

'And then what?' protested Zach. 'Tell the agency that based on drunken statements made and proof shown to me, they all had tattoos matching the symbol left at the crime scenes? Even if it's incriminating enough, there would be a whole process to go through. With good lawyers, perhaps appeals for less time, parole? No, that wasn't good enough.'

Zach pointed at himself. 'I promised myself the day Kieth died I would hunt down and bring those murderers to justice. And then I promised it again when I learnt they'd killed Harry and you had wrongly convicted Kieth. You were so down on yourself for your mistake, but it wasn't *your* mistake, it was *them* who ensured they would not be caught.'

Luke listened to Zach, then he asked the question that lay heavily on his heart. 'Zach, this . . . us . . . was it just to—'

'No. It was never to advance my mission or to use you. Luke, it was unexpected – us – and I was conflicted at first, but I love you.' Zach creased his brows. 'I fell in love with you long before I knew you had convicted Kieth. That was what had me in turmoil.' Zach heaved a sob. 'I did this for *us*. I did it for *them*, for Kieth and Harry.'

Zach took a step forward. 'Luke, I thought my life had ended the day Kieth died. But then I vowed to find those killers, and I joined the agency so I could find them and kill them without getting caught. But I did not want to hide this from you anymore – my intent, or what I had done. Because despite the promise I made to avenge Kieth's death, my life had renewed purpose when we shared our first kiss.'

Zach reached for Luke's hand. 'I fell in love with you and I have loved you for the past decade. I will continue to love you no matter what.'

Zach unclipped his gun and placed it on a table beside them. 'What happens now is up to you, Luke. I'm ready for my life to end here, because you might convict me or shoot a murderer. But my purpose is fulfilled.' He pressed his lips in a line as fresh tears fell streamed down his face. He whispered, 'My love for you will never cease.'

In that moment, Luke knew what had to be done.

* * *

Zach stared at Luke, now unarmed, having said his peace, hoping Luke at least believed his love to be true. Zach cursed himself for sounding like a generic sob story, but it was genuine. And if his life ended here, at least he'll have come clean to the man he loved.

Luke took a few steps back suddenly. Fear gripped Zach, his heart sinking as Luke's face became twisted with contempt. The older man reached into his kit and donned his gloves before pulling out an evidence bag. Luke bent to pick up the note . . . and then lit a lighter and burned the note, letting the ashes fall into the evidence bag. The final cinders burnt out, leaving only ashes behind from what once had been the fourth note.

Zach had to wonder what Luke was doing. His heart was pounding so fast.

Luke pulled his phone out. Zach sighed, looking down. He was calling it in – of course, he would. Luke was one to follow the rules more than Zach ever was.

'Melinda,' said Luke, 'we found the fourth vic. A murderer too. I think . . . this is the end of the line. Four on four now found and . . . no note.'

Zach gaped at Luke, eyes wide in surprise.

Luke concluded. 'I think whoever our killer is, they're done . . . Got it.'

Luke put his phone away.

'I don't understand.' Zach shook his head. 'I'm a murderer.'

'No, you're not. Not like them. Else you wouldn't have spiralled.' Luke retrieved his gun and holstered it. He walked over to Zach and took his hands in his. 'We lost men we loved because of the justice system's flaws. And because of the law's flaws, you would get sent down. But you provided justice.'

Luke cupped Zach's face with his gloved hand. 'Zach, I'm not losing another man I love. We both know what that loss feels like.'

Zach felt like he was in a dream. He breathed out shakily.

'I'm not losing you, Zach.' Luke's voice cracked and his eyes filled with tears. 'I don't ever want to lose you.' Zach let out a sob. 'So I will bear this burden of secrecy with you, and we will both know that the deaths of the men we loved – of the man I had dedicated my life to – have been avenged . . . by the man I am ready to dedicate my life to.'

Zach breathed in sharply.

Luke offered him a tender smile. 'I do want to.' Both of them breathed out sobs. 'I do want to marry you, Zach.'

Luke got down on one knee. Zach couldn't help but let out a small laugh at the circumstances of the proposal.

Luke smiled up at Zach, earnest and hopeful. 'You said your future is in my hands. Then take my hand. Let this be a renewal, a new start – together. I want your future to be with me, by my side. Zachary, will you marry me?'

Zach laughed tearfully, overcome with all the emotions of the day. 'Yes.'

He pulled Luke to his feet and kissed him deeply. Luke pulled away all too soon and leaned his forehead on Zach's.

'Let's finish up in here before the team arrives,' said Luke.

And they did, ensuring no evidence of the destruction of the last note was left behind.

Luke reached for Zach's hand and interlaced their fingers. He brought their hands close to his heart. 'I love you, Zach,' he whispered.

'I love you, Luke.' Zach was awed by Luke's decision.

'Thank you for bringing justice to those who took Harry from me. Thank you for accepting to be my new husband.'

'Thank you for accepting what I've done. Thank you for not fearing me now that you know.'

Once the adrenaline of it all had passed and Zach was visiting the scenes of his crimes, he had found it difficult to maintain his composure. What had made it worse was keeping it from Luke. But they had seen the justice done now, and Zach could let go. He was free, as was Luke.

Luke brought Zach in close. 'I know that I will always be safe with you, because you won't let anyone hurt me. And if they did, you would hunt them down. I . . . *want* that dedication from a man.' Luke looked away sheepishly.

'You *have* that dedication from me,' asserted Zach. 'I will never let anyone take you away from me.'

'Good, because I promise the same.'

Zach kissed Luke tenderly, fresh tears stinging his eyes. He was so grateful in that moment, and as though Luke knew his thoughts, he said,

'I am so grateful towards you for what you have done for us.' Luke stared fondly at Zach, understanding passing between them from all the revelations. Luke handed Zach his gun back. 'Now let's go report back to Melinda so we can go shop for engagement rings.'

Zach's heart soared.

Hands interlaced, Zach and Luke left the final crime scene where justice had been completed, leaving behind their pasts and the secrets only *they* harboured, both ready to move forward . . . together.

* * *

A drunken night led to boasting of hidden tattoos.

Looking deeper into it led to the truth.

All four have been found and confirmed.

Now justice has been made for the men they took from us.

<u>THANK YOU SO MUCH FOR READING</u>

If you enjoyed this story,
please consider taking a few moments
to write a review on Amazon or Goodreads.
It would mean so much.

Thank you.

Please enjoy this passage from

Sanguine Sincerity

The first book in an ongoing series of
Supernatural LGBTQ Erotic Romance Thriller
books.

THE EXCERPT IS CLEAN.

Warnings:
Strong language, violence and blood.

<u>CHAPTER ONE</u>

Present Day.

The silence was both terrifying and soothing at the same time. Liam closed his eyes and leaned against the brick wall as he stood outside the club. It had been busy, with people dancing, shouting, laughing, all drunkenly. Now, the stillness of the winter night dampened whatever sounds came from the boulevard a few streets down.

This was where he had often stood with Julian after their work shifts, talking, laughing, kissing, and making plans for their future together. But Julian was gone, left before dawn a few nights after they had declared their love for each other, left without a word or explanation. Only a scribble on a sticky note saying, *'I have to leave. I'm sorry.'*

It hurt, it still did, even after all these weeks. Julian had never called or answered Liam's calls or texts after that night; Julian had simply disappeared from Liam's life. Liam didn't understand why – he thought they'd been happy.

He had once relished in the quiet after the bustle of work, now he missed hearing Julian's voice or seeing his smile. His heart broke every day again and again. Yet he continued to stand here in the spot they had made theirs.

Liam couldn't help but wonder if things had moved too fast between them – no, he had declared his love six full months after they'd met and started dating. He was just so confused about it all.

Taking a deep breath, he ensured the club was well locked and began down the dark alley. He didn't want to linger too long. There had been murders in the neighbourhood in recent weeks, all gunshot wounds. The rival gangs were at it again. It hadn't stopped the clubgoers, though. Liam figured it was only a matter of time before both mobs decided they wanted to own the club and took their fight to the neighbouring streets.

Liam heard the screech of tires and shouting not too far. He paused, waiting to make sure it was just some drunk folks, but he tensed when he heard a gunshot pierce the stillness.

Looks like the gang fight's here now, he thought to himself.

He quickened his pace and veered the corner into the next alley and came face to face with the man who had left him.

'Julian!' Liam breathed. He swallowed hard, his heart suddenly drumming in his chest.

'Liam.' Julian hesitated. His blue eyes seemed brighter in the darkness of the night and the light in the alley gave his already pale complexion a blue hue, making his handsome features that much more intense, increasing the yearning and anguish in Liam's heart.

Liam was flooded by a wave of emotions. 'What the hell, Julian?' he shouted, tears stinging his eyes.

Julian winced, chagrined, and Liam saw his eyes sparkle with tears.

'Look,' began Julian, taking a step towards Liam, 'I know I owe you an explanation, I just . . . You need to get out of here. I came to get you to safety.'

Liam took a step back, putting two and two together. 'I know what this is,' he seethed. 'You're with the mafias, aren't you?'

'No, I swear, Liam! I'm not with them,' protested Julian. 'I heard about the Cromwells and Sharpes taking their fight here and I came to warn you. Liam, please.' Julian reached for Liam's hand.

Liam pulled away out of reach. 'A little convenient, isn't it?'

Julian grimaced. 'Liam, I promise you—'

'Promise me? I told you I loved you and then you ran!' shouted Liam, his voice hoarse with heartache. His heart felt tight, and it hurt all over again.

Julian merely gaped at him.

'I thought you loved me too,' Liam wept.

'I do. I do *still* love you,' insisted Julian.

'Then why did you leave?' demanded Liam.

'I had . . . priorities.' He caught himself. 'Sorry, that sounds . . . I had . . . a mission.'

'A mission?' Liam repeated, incredulous. 'Crime mission? Or are you with the cops?'

'None of those,' admitted Julian. 'Look, I promise I'll explain everything. Let's just get out of here, go somewhere safe, and I'll explain everything.' He paused and a tear trickled down his cheek – he wiped it away with the back of his thumb. 'I just ask that you trust me.'

'You left, Julian.' The tightness in Liam's chest squeezed harder. 'You claim you love me but you left – why come back now?'

Julian stared at Liam, eyes pleading. 'I had no choice, something . . . took me away for a while, and I realise I should have told you then what it was and why that was, because—'

Gunshot thundering too close for comfort interrupted their tearful exchange.

Julian grabbed Liam's hand and began to run, pulling Liam along with him. 'We have to get out of here. I'm not going to let any harm come to you.'

'Oh, how noble!' spat Liam.

Julian spun on Liam, glaring at him. 'I came back as soon as my mission was complete. I always intended to. I just couldn't tell you then and it's . . . difficult to explain, it would be difficult for you to belie—'

With surprising speed, Julian placed his hand in front of Liam and pushed him against the wall, backing up as a bullet whizzed past them.

Liam stared at Julian, mouth agape. 'Thanks.'

Julian took a beat, looking alarmed, before grabbing hold of Liam's hand again and guiding him out of the alley and bolting onto the street. Shouts coming from nearby told them which way *not* to run as they turned onto the next street over, darting as fast as they could.

Some of the mobsters ran onto the street where they were. Julian skidded to a stop, his eyes darting this way and that, looking hypervigilant. He grabbed Liam's arm and pulled him close, turning around as one of the gang members took aim at them. They ducked behind a parked car.

'We're not with the Sharpes!' Julian shouted. Liam noted how Julian had easily recognised that the ones shooting at them were the Cromwells.

In response, the shooter reloaded his gun.

'Shit!' Julian cursed. He looked towards another parked car. 'If we can get ourselves out of this area,' he told Liam, 'then we—'

The window of the car behind which they hid shattered as another shot resounded behind them.

They ran towards the next car, and then towards another building. Another thunderous roar broke the air as more gang members began shooting at each other. Liam and Julian's assailant continued after them and just as they came up to hide in an alcove, a bullet hit Julian with a thud.

He cried out in pain, bringing his hand to his arm.

'Julian!' Liam cried.

Julian closed his eyes, wincing. 'I'll be fine,' he gritted. He looked over at Liam as they leaned against the wall. 'I'm sorry I never told you the truth. I'm sorry

I left – I'm sorry I hurt you. But I swear I love you and I will tell you *everything*. We just need to get to safety.'

Liam nodded. 'You knew they were coming here. I just can't wrap my head around—'

'I found out just hours ago.' Julian looked at his wound, breathing deeply but looking like the pain wasn't as intense now as it was before. 'I got myself here as quickly as I could.'

'You came to . . . warn me . . .' Liam was just so confused. 'Please, tell me if you're part of a gang of some sort.'

'Of some sort,' Julian repeated pensively. 'Not a mafia, no. Not a . . . It's complicated.' Julian pinched his fingers and reached into his wound and pulled out the bullet with nothing more than a small groan. 'I'm good.'

Suddenly, the barrel of a handgun emerged from the corner – the shooter was pointing it straight at Julian's head, his grip on the handgun firm and steady.

Liam froze.

Julian stared the other man in the eyes. 'Big mistake,' he sneered.

With exceptional speed, he grabbed the assailant's arm, pulling and twisting. The Cromwell crony cried out, dropping the gun, and Julian grabbed his neck and twisted hard. The man fell dead on the ground before him.

Liam stared at Julian. 'And you say you're not a cop or with a mob,' he said, unconvinced. He pointed at the dead shooter, his eyes never leaving Julian's. 'Explain that!'

'Not here.'

Julian picked up the dead man's gun and began to run; Liam followed close behind. A car turned onto the street and mobsters began to shoot at anyone who was nearby.

'Fuck!' Julian shouted. Shielding Liam as they continued to run, Julian took aim and began shooting at the mobsters within the vehicle, hitting his mark every time.

'Now I know there's definitely something you're not telling me,' Liam muttered as they ran.

'There is, and I promise I'll tell you,' replied Julian. He secured the clip and aimed afresh, again not missing his target.

Liam's throat and lungs were burning but he pushed forward. They turned another corner as the car behind them crashed into a fence.

Liam stopped before Julian, facing him. 'The truth now, Julian!'

Panting, Julian stared at Liam. 'We need to get away from here,' he insisted.

'I'm not moving until you tell me what's going on.'

Fear flashed in Julian's eyes. 'You're not going to believe me without the full explanation.'

'Then quit stalling and explain already!' demanded Liam.

Julian worked his jaw. 'I'm—'

A deafening gunshot exploded – Liam felt a sharp, burning sensation in his gut, and his knees buckled beneath him as he struggled to stay upright.

'No!' screamed Julian.

He caught Liam before he could hit the ground, gently setting him down. Liam's breath came out syncopated as he realised what had just happened. He screamed in pain – a loud guttural scream – then winced, clenching his jaw.

'No, no, this is what I was trying to prevent,' Julian quavered, opening up Liam's jacket and staring at the wound. 'I can't lose you.'

'Lose me? You left me.'

Julian let out a tearful breath. 'I left on a mission I couldn't tell you about. I'm so sorry, Liam.'

Liam glanced down at his stomach as his blood rapidly drenched his clothes. Seeing it only made his heart pump harder and the blood gush faster, and Liam's breath came out shakily.

Julian pulled Liam close to his chest, picking him up off the ground, and began to run. Liam didn't know if it was the dizziness of blood loss that altered his perceptions but he felt like they were moving a lot faster than was normal. He saw houses whizz by his vision and then trees as they entered the forest. The sounds of guns and shouting mobsters grew distant until, finally, the quiet of the night was all that remained.

Julian placed Liam down on the snow, which quickly turned red from his blood. Julian's jaw was clenched.

The pain Liam felt was immeasurable, yet somehow he couldn't bring himself to scream again, and he was so sweat-soaked from fear, he barely noticed the cold.

'I should never have waited this long to tell you the truth, Liam.' Julian looked down at Liam's wound, his tears dripping onto it.

Liam tried to speak but a mere whimper escaped him as tears stung his eyes.

Julian's voice came out determined yet half-whispered. 'I'm not going to let you die.'

'I think,' Liam winced, his voice laboured, 'it's too late for that.'

'No!' Something flashed in Julian's eyes. Liam lifted a bloodied hand to Julian's face; Julian placed his hand on his. 'I came back because I love you . . . because I owe you the truth. So here is the truth.'

His eyes flashed again and paled, brightening, his pupils becoming as blue as his irises and nearly as pale. He let his mouth hang open, and smoothly his top canines extended. Liam's eyes widened and he gaped at Julian.

'You're a—' he gasped.

'Yes. I can save your life, but tell me no and I won't, as much as that grieves me. I won't force this life on you.'

Liam gritted his teeth as a wave of pain threatened to pull him into unconsciousness. 'Do it!'

Julian leaned down towards him and gently placed his teeth on his skin. He paused. Liam felt Julian's breath on his neck before an intense sting.

He winced, grabbing Julian's arm tightly. He felt Julian's lips wrap around the punctures and the pain eased. As Julian sucked his blood, Liam relaxed in his caress.

Julian kissed Liam's neck tenderly before pulling away. 'It's done,' he said softly.

Liam waited, his body trembling lightly. Then he began to shake, but not from pain, from some sort of power that coursed through his veins. It was a vibration that came from inside of him that he felt gushing through all his veins. In his mouth, Liam felt his eyeteeth extend, and there was a mild prickle in his eyes that he just knew was the same kind of flare he'd seen in Julian's eyes.

Liam looked down at his wound, feeling an uncomfortable sensation. The bullet appeared at the opening of the hole in his stomach and fell out. Then the wound closed and Liam felt himself heal inside his body. It wasn't pleasant but the discomfort quickly passed.

Liam swallowed hard, breathing in deeply. He stared at Julian.

He wasn't sure which of them sprung towards the other first but their lips met and their mouths opened to let the other in, and they kissed fervently. The familiar tingling in Liam's stomach told him how much he loved and wanted Julian.

He pulled away. Julian leaned his forehead on his.

'I am so sorry, Liam, that I never told you the truth.'

'You should have trusted that I'd believe you,' Liam placed his hand on Julian's face, 'that I'd still love you despite who or what you are.' Liam grimaced at the blood he'd smeared on Julian who didn't seem to mind.

Julian kissed Liam again. 'I love you, Liam. I promise I'll never leave your side again.'

Liam let that sink in, realising the implications of this new situation. 'I guess that means we're geared to spend eternity together.'

Julian's lips quirked into a side grin. 'Is that a proposal?'

Liam chuckled, feeling flutters all over his body. 'It is if you want it to be.'

Julian beamed at him, and with his heightened senses Liam could feel the truth and their love reverberate and pulse between them.

Liam pressed a long and ardent kiss to Julian's lips, wrapping his arms around him, deepening the kiss with each passing moment, and his tongue traced his lover's vampiric canines as they hungrily devoured each other's mouths.

Liam drew back and met Julian's gaze. 'You owe me one hell of an explanation.'

Julian let out a small laugh. 'That, I do.'

Julian helped Liam to his feet and he beckoned him to follow. He held out his hand and Liam took it, interlacing their fingers. They walked through the snow in the forest, the silence of the night no longer terrifying Liam, and Julian's voice soothingly cut through the stillness as he began his story.

Also By

Also Written by Eidahs

Sanguine Sincerity
(https://binkyproductions.com/supernaturalromance)

The Thief and His Hunter Book 1
(https://binkyproductions.com/TheThiefandHisHunter)

Like Father, Not Like Sons
Legacy Takedown
Of Sullied Dreams and Beaten Hearts
Butchery At the Debauchery
Serendipitous Tribulation
(https://binkyproductions.com/shortstories)

Also Published by Binky Ink

Stardust Destinies I: Variate Facing
Stardust Destinies II: The Drought
(https://binkyproductions.com/stardustdestinies)

The Hidden Cove: Pirate's Misadventure
(https://binkyproductions.com/shortstories)

Eidahs is a pseudonym for all mature written works, from thrillers to erotic romance. Eidahs in pronunciation sounds elven in nature, which is why she chose it, to tap into her love of fantasy, a genre that couples well with super-natural and preternatural, dark fantasy, and romance.

Eidahs is also the nickname 'Shadie' backwards, repre-senting the shadow self, innermost desires, and a spectrum of emotions, most notably, passion, sorrow, rage, and delight, which Eidahs loves to incorporate in her writing. Enticing readers and evoking the characters' emotions when she writes has guided her inspiration to spell many short stories on Medium and a series of books under this pen name.

Connect with Binky Ink:

WordPress Website & Blog
    https://binkyproductions.com/binkyinkwriting
Medium – Main Profile
    https://medium.com/@BinkyInkWriting
X (Twitter) https://twitter.com/binkyinkwriting